WHEN I AM
HAPPIEST

When I am happiest

WRITTEN BY
Rose Lagercrantz

ILLUSTRATED BY
Eva Eriksson

GECKO PRESS

CONTENTS

Chapter 1

It's the second-to-last day of Dani's first year at school.

Dani's so happy she could write a book about it!

In fact, that's exactly what she's done, but unfortunately it's not quite finished yet.

The question is whether it ever will be.

Now the book is in her backpack with all the other things she has to take home before the summer break.

The only thing not yet in the backpack is the photo of Dani's best friend in the whole world, Ella.

This year, Ella moved to another town, thousands of roads and forests and houses away.

Dani has had her photo on her desk since Ella left. She's looked at it so many times it should have completely faded away.

But luckily you can't make photos fade just by looking at them.

Every time Dani looks at the picture, Ella gives her a fresh smile.

This time too.

And Dani smiles back. Then she puts the photo in her backpack.

Now she's almost finished with school for the year.

In the morning it will be the very last day of school, when everyone has to put on their best clothes and sing. Dani's going to wear the new dress her grandmother bought her.

In the shop there were two dresses Dani liked: one pale blue and one with pink stripes.

She didn't know which one to choose.

In the end, she sang:

Eeny, meeny, miny, moe,
Catch a tiger by the toe.
If he hollers, let him go.
Eeny, meeny…
miny…
moe!

It was the blue one!

She also got new white sandals with roses on the toes.

Chapter 2

Not only do the children have to wear their best clothes for the last day, but the classroom has to be decorated too.

All morning the class has been busy painting flowers and hanging them on the walls.

Dani painted a big purple rose. It was really beautiful! Everyone who saw it thought so.

But by the time it was ready to hang, the thumbtacks had run out.

It looked as if Dani's flower wouldn't be on the wall.

At the last second, Vicky and Mickey came to the rescue.

"You can have this one," said Vicky, pulling a thumbtack out of her shoe.

Mickey pulled one out too and gave it to Dani.

Mickey and Vicky often have thumbtacks in their shoes because it makes them sound like tap dancers.

"Oh, thank you!" said Dani.

"No problem," said Vicky.

"That's what friends are for," said Mickey.

The teacher had told them they should all try to be friends. And they are, Vicky says.

Best friends, says Mickey.

But one day when they played ghost ball and
Dani happened to win…

Vicky and Mickey were so angry they chased
her till she crashed into an older girl called Ellen…

and Dani
hurt her nose so
badly it almost fell off!
   Ellen said sorry over and over again.

But Vicky said:
"That's nothing much!"
And Mickey thought so too.
Best friends aren't always the kindest.
That's something Dani has learned.

Chapter 3

But overall it's been a good year.

Especially the time Suzy pretended to be a cow.

That was during Fun Hour.

Dani laughed so much her stomach hurt.

And there was the time the teacher told a story about a little boy who floated down the river Nile in a basket.

And she showed them old pictures from when she was their age. About a hundred years ago.

The boy was named Moses. Dani loves that story!

Imagine something as wonderful as a little boy floating in a basket in the reeds!

When Moses grew up he went up a mountain and met God who gave him the Ten Commandments. They were written on two stone tablets.

The commandments were rules that people should follow so that everything would work out happily.

Then Dani and Ella made their own commandments—because back then Ella was still in Dani's class.

Dani and Ella wrote their commandments on thick pieces of paper because they didn't have stone tablets.

Their first commandment was:

You should never hit someone smaller than you.

If a little child is very upset you should leave it alone until it has calmed down.

Their second commandment:

You shouldn't show off too much.

Only a little bit, if someone else is showing off a lot. For example, if someone says: "My bike's better than yours!"

That's what Cushion says, even though his bike is so old it hardly hangs together.

His grandfather has fixed it at least ten times.

The third commandment went:

Don't be greedy!

If there are thirty cakes and a hundred people want to try them, don't eat all the cakes yourself!

Writing commandments was fun!

Back when Ella was in the class it was always fun, except one time when they had to draw pictures of their mothers.

Dani can't remember very much from the years when she had a mother. She was so little then. She can only remember them telling her that her mother had died.

Her father cried.

Years later, he told Dani the last thing her mother had said:

"Say goodbye from me, especially to Dani," she had told him.

That felt good to know.

When they had to draw pictures of their mothers, Dani drew her father instead.

MY FATHER

Chapter 4

Dani is a happy person, she really is—but not all the time.

She tries not to think about the unhappy times. She'd rather skip over them.

In any case, she doesn't cry much anymore. She's getting quite big. More like her father. And he never cries. Only when someone dies.

Something else new about Dani is that she has had her ears pierced.

At first she didn't dare. But her father came
with her and held her hand.

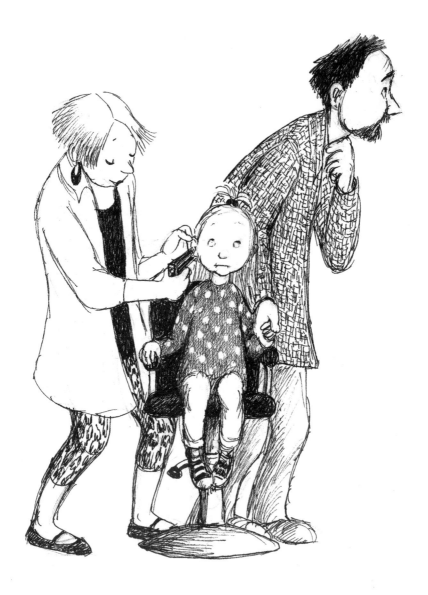

And soon she had small glass diamonds in her
ears. She only has to touch them to feel happy.

That's what she's doing for the last hour of the
second-to-last day of school.

Because she's the first one finished with packing her things, she gets to write a story.

But it has to be a quick one.

THE TERRIBLE ISLAND

That's what it's called. It's about a girl who walks around an island picking flowers.

"Good," says the teacher when she has read it, "but what was terrible about it?"

"I don't know," says Dani. "Something terrible was supposed to happen, but it never did! Just like always."

"That's nice," says the teacher. "But now I think you should find a good ending for your masterpiece!"

Dani knows very well what her teacher is talking about.

She means the book about Dani's happy life. The one that isn't finished yet and is packed away in her backpack.

Dani picks the backpack up from the floor and finds the book. She opens it to the first empty page near the back. What should go on it?

In such a happy book, the ending should be the happiest part of all.

Dani thinks for a bit. She thinks so hard that you can hear her brain creaking.

That's what you say even though it's completely quiet when you do it. The quietest you can ever be is when you're thinking so hard that your brain creaks.

What should she write?

The problem is that Dani is happy so often that it's hard to choose.

Vicky and Mickey are happy when they have birthdays and get presents.

Cushion is happy when he plays football and scores the winning goal. Meatball is too.

But Dani is happy about almost everything.

Even the time her class lost their baseball game,
Dani was happy. Really happy!

Afterwards Cushion said:

"Everyone who thinks this was fun, put up your
hand!"

Dani's hand was the only one that went up.

But that isn't a thing she wants to write about.

Soon she thinks of something better and picks up her pen.

The last time I was happiest, she begins.

She gets no further before the classroom door opens.

Bee—who usually works in the principal's office—pops her head in. She only comes to the classroom when something special has happened.

Now she waves to the teacher.

The teacher hurries out and closes the door behind her. But soon it opens again.

"Dani, can you come here, please?" says the teacher. Her voice sounds strange.

Has Dani done something wrong? What could it be?

Dani puts down her pen and gets up. Her knees feel quite wobbly.

Everyone watches her as she goes out into the hall.

Chapter 5

The teacher gives Dani a serious look.

She can be strict. Although there's usually always a twinkle in her eyes. But not now. Now they are plain gray.

"Today your grandmother is coming to pick you up," she says.

Dani looks questioningly at her.

Grandma quite often comes to pick Dani up after school, for example on Fridays when they go to the swimming pool.

But this is Wednesday.

The teacher takes Dani's hands.

"There's been an accident…" she begins.

Dani turns cold. Icy cold.

The teacher hesitates a moment.

"Your father has been run over," she continues.

Dani begins to tremble.

"He was biking to work."

The teacher looks as if she's about to say more, but she doesn't.

Dani's schoolmates, who have been creeping
out into the corridor, wonder what's happening.
Bee tries to stop them, but she can't.

"Bee," says the teacher finally, "stay here with
Dani, and I'll go and talk to the class."

Bee takes off her big cardigan and puts it around Dani's shoulders.

And Dani sinks onto the school bench beneath the coat hangers and shuts her eyes.

There was something she had to remember!

What was it?

Something she was thinking just before she was interrupted.

"The last time I was happiest," she mumbles to herself. Then her mind goes blank.

Chapter 6

It's not long before Dani's grandmother arrives.
She hugs Dani long and hard.

"There, there," she says.

Then she tries to explain what has happened.
But Dani doesn't want to hear. She puts her
hands over her ears and keeps them there until
Grandma stops talking.

Then Dani whispers:

"Where is he?"

"In the hospital," says Grandma. "Come on,
we'll go now."

They leave the school in silence.

When they're almost at the car they hear the
bell ring. Dani stops and turns around. Some
of her schoolmates are running down the steps.
They wave to her.

But Dani doesn't wave back.

"Come on now, Dani," says Grandma.

Dani stays where she is.

"What are you waiting for?"

Dani doesn't answer. She can't. She doesn't know what she's waiting for. She is completely bewildered.

Then the teacher appears. She is carrying something.

"Your backpack, Dani!" she calls.

Grandma hurries back to get it.

"Thank you," she says, "and thank you for all you've done this year!"

Grandma and the teacher continue talking.

After a while the teacher comes over to Dani and gives her a big envelope.

"All your classmates are thinking of you. These are letters from some who were quick enough to write you a few lines."

"That's very kind," says Grandma.

But Dani doesn't say a word.

When Grandma goes on to the car, Dani stumbles after her.

She climbs into the car and puts on her seat belt.

She doesn't open her mouth until they've driven quite a long way.

"We're going to see Dad now, aren't we?" she asks in a croaky voice.

"No," says Grandma. "We're going to your house. We'll gather up the cat and the hamsters. We'll be looking after you for a few days."

"But I have to see Dad," Dani protests.

"You can't see him yet," says Grandma. "He's asleep."

"Then we should go and wake him up!"

"I'm afraid we can't. He's so deeply asleep that he can't be woken yet," explains Grandma.

It's quiet in the car.

"But what if he never…" begins Dani.

She stops. She mustn't think that!

But this time she can't help it.

Dani has found something she can't not think.

She crumples up in the back seat.

Chapter 7

When they arrive at Dani's house, she gets out of the car and follows Grandma to the door.

But Dani doesn't want to go inside.

She stops in front of the house and looks around.

In the morning when she went to school everything was normal.

But now her whole life has turned upside down.

The only thing still the same is the blue dress. It's hanging on its coat hanger, waiting for the end of school as if nothing has happened. And the shoes, the ones with roses on the toes, are waiting as well.

The cat comes and purrs, standing completely still with its nose in the air as if it's asking what the matter is.

But Dani doesn't feel like telling.

Grandma takes the dress off its hanger and lays it carefully in a bag with the shoes.

Then she collects the cage with Snow and Flake and puts it down in front of Dani.

Two terrified hamsters look out from the cage.

What's going on?

Dani takes the cage, and Grandma takes Cat
and the suitcase. Then they leave the house.

Dani stops at the gate and looks back.

"Goodbye, house," she mumbles.

"Soon they'll call from the hospital to tell us that Dad's woken up," says Grandma when they're back in the car.

But you can tell she's not absolutely sure.

Chapter 8

And what happens next?

Not very much.

Dani paces about in Grandma and Grandpa's house, waiting for the phone to ring.

Grandma stays in the kitchen, putting away glasses and plates. Grandpa sits paralyzed behind his newspaper in the sitting room.

Dani touches the envelope the teacher gave her,
but she doesn't open it.

Right now she can't read any letters.

All she can do is wait.

She doesn't leave the telephone for a moment.
Not even with her eyes.

The phone doesn't ring, but the doorbell does and
Dani's cousin Sven looks in.

He and his mother live nearby, so he visits
Grandma and Grandpa almost every day.

"You're here!" he cries happily when he sees Dani.

"Yes," Dani sighs.

Sven looks at her in surprise.

"It's good you came!" calls Grandma from the
kitchen. And Grandpa looks out from behind his
newspaper.

"Hello, Sven! Can you and Dani find something
fun to do together?"

"Of course," says Sven. "Come on, Dani, let's
go to my house and say hello to Tiger!"

Sven loves animals. His dream is to have a dog,
preferably a wolfhound, which only he can tame.
But so far he has to make do with a parakeet, one
with tiger-stripes on its front.

That's why it's called Tiger.

"I'm teaching Tiger to talk," he says. "That bird is a genius…"

He stops and looks at the envelope Dani has pushed away over the table.

"TO DANI," he reads.

"It's letters to Dani from her classmates," Grandpa explains.

"From her classmates? Why would they write to her?"

Dani doesn't answer.

"Shall I open it for you?"

Without waiting for an answer, he tears open the envelope with his finger and holds it upside down.

Several pieces of paper fall out.

One of them is decorated with suns, another with footballs, a third with skulls.

Sven studies them closely.

"Dani!" he bursts out. "These are very strange. Listen to this!"

Hi Dani!
I will think of you over the summer.
With best wishes from Meatball

Sven looks questioningly at Dani, but she looks away.

He reads the next piece of paper:

GO DANI! GO DANI!
From Benni
P. S. GO DANI!

Then comes a letter from Cushion:

HI DANI!
I HOPE YOUR FATHER GETS
BETTER SO YOU DON'T HAVE
TO GO TO AN ORPHANAGE!

Dani sniffs, even though she doesn't cry any more these days. Sven puts down the letters and looks at Grandpa.

"Would someone like to tell me what's happened?"

Grandpa straightens up.

"Dani's father has been run over," he says.

"Run over!" Sven shrieks. "How?"

"By a car when he was biking to work."

"Is he very…run over?" Sven asks.

"We don't know. He's unconscious. We're waiting to hear from the hospital."

Sven sinks into the sofa and stares intently at the telephone with the others. But it stays silent.

In the end Grandpa picks up the phone and makes a call.

"Can I speak to someone in intensive care?" he asks.

Then he goes out into the hall.

"They say his condition is unchanged," he says when he comes back.

"What does that mean?" asks Sven.

"That nothing new has happened."

"I want to see Dad anyway," says Dani.

"Soon you'll be able to." Grandpa tries to calm her. "As soon as he wakes up."

Then Sven says what mustn't be said, let alone thought. "But what if he never does? What if Dani's father never wakes up?"

Dani starts bawling her eyes out.

Grandpa takes out a big red handkerchief and wipes Dani's nose.

"Calm down, Dani!" he tries to say.

But Dani can't calm down. She cries as she's never cried before, loudly and so hard that Grandpa can't bear it.

"I want to see my Dad!" bawls Dani.

Grandpa gives in. "Come on, let's go then,"
he says.

Chapter 9

And so it is that Dani, on the second-to-last day of school, goes to the hospital where her father lies sleeping so deeply that he might never wake up again.

She cries all the way there.

She cries all the way down the long hospital corridors.

She can't stop even when they reach intensive care.

First Grandpa speaks to the doctor. Then the doctor turns to Dani.

"Are you sure you want to see your father right now? You might feel scared. He has lots of tubes in him!"

At last Dani stops crying.

"No," she sniffs and wipes away tears with the back of her hand. "I won't be scared."

"Dani is very brave," Grandpa agrees.

And the doctor takes her hand as they go into the room where her father is.

But she is scared, nonetheless, when she sees him.

Her father is lying absolutely still with his eyes closed, surrounded by machines that blink and beep.

It's a long while before Dani dares to let go of the doctor's hand and go over to the bed.

"Dad," she whispers.

But he doesn't move.

"Your father can't hear what you say," the doctor explains.

"Dad," says Dani, louder this time.

Dad doesn't move.

Dani takes a breath and shouts in her loudest voice: "WAKE UP, DAD! IT'S DANI!"

And then it happens! His face moves a little and he opens his eyes.

"Dani..." he mumbles.

Then he mumbles something else: *"Amore!"*

That's Italian, because Dani's father is from Italy. And *amore* means love in Italian.

After he's said it, he closes his eyes. Dani turns anxiously to the doctor and the nurse.

"Has he gone back to sleep?"

"Yes," says the doctor. "But he woke up. And he knew you immediately! That is a very good sign."

The doctor turns to Grandpa. "But it will be some time before he's all better."

"How long?"

"Probably the whole summer."

"The whole summer!" cries Dani.

"Don't be sad!" Grandpa is quick to comfort her. "You can stay with us. And have fun with Sven. And with me!"

Dani tries to swallow her disappointment.

Yes. She will have fun with Sven. And help him teach Tiger to talk.

And help Grandpa with his stamp collection.

Dani's grandpa is a stamp collector. But not just any old stamps. Only the most valuable ones in the world. And stamps with sports on them.

Dani's a collector, too. But only of stamps with whales on them, because they're in danger of extinction.

When she thinks about how badly in danger whales are, she almost starts crying again.

She doesn't usually cry any more, but today she's crying over all kinds of things.

Chapter 10

As soon as they get home to Grandma and Sven, Grandpa tells them what Dani has done:

"She just went up to her father and ordered him to wake up!"

He describes how amazed they were, both he and the doctor.

Grandma's amazed too when she hears what happened.

And Sven's so impressed that he doesn't say a thing for a long time.

It's not until dinnertime that he becomes himself again, tapping his glass and standing up, as people do when they're about to make a speech.

"You have to guess a riddle," he says, because Sven always has a couple of riddles up his sleeve.

This one goes: "How many eyes does a herring have?"

He waits a moment so they can think.

"Well?"

Grandma guesses two.

"Wrong," says Sven, pleased.

"Surely it has two," says Grandpa.

"Still wrong!"

Then Dani puts up her hand as if she's at school.

"One," she says, because she's heard that riddle before. It happens to be Ella's best joke.

"Right," says Sven.

"What!" cries Grandpa. "Only one?"

"Yes, because herring only has one i!" Sven crows.

When Sven has eaten dinner and emptied the bowl of M&Ms on the table beside the sofa, he disappears back to his own house.

And Dani fetches her hamsters, whom she's hardly had a chance to see all day.

"The worst is over now," she tells them. "Come on, let's go outside!"

Chapter 11

With her hamsters in her arms, Dani sits on the bench outside. That's where she and Sven used to sit and hold hands when they were small.

And they would sing:

Dani and Sven
sitting in a tree,
K-I-S-S-I-N-G!

But that was a long time ago. That was when they were living with Grandpa and Grandma almost the whole time, because Dani's mother was sick.

"There, there," she says to Snow and Flake. "At last I have time to talk to you. I'll try and tell you what's happened…"

The hamsters creep into her lap and get ready to listen.

But there's not actually much to say. Dani doesn't feel like talking. She's worried that her dad has gone deep asleep again.

She tries to think about something else. Ella, for example. But she can't.

Today she can't think about anything except her father.

Grandma comes out onto the steps.

"Dani," she says. "Do you think you could pick some flowers for your teacher?"

Dani nods. Perhaps she should give the teacher a present as well. But what? A book…

Suddenly she knows which one: *My happy life*.

Her teacher thinks it's so special, that book.

But if it's going to be a present it has to be finished!

Just as she gets up from the bench, she hears someone call her name.

It's old Jimmy coming with his dog.

Jimmy's knees are so sore sometimes that he has trouble walking, but the dog is bouncy and needs exercise.

Now it's heading straight for Dani and the hamsters.

"Dani, would you be so kind as to walk my dog?" asks Jimmy, sinking down on the bench. "I have to rest my weary bones."

Dani nods and leaves Snow and Flake with
Grandma. Then she rushes after the dog to a
corner of the woods where lilies of the valley grow.

Lilies of the valley are one of the things Dani loves best.

The scent! She can't help being a little bit happy when she smells it. But is that all right, when your dad has just been run over?

The walk makes her feel better. She has always liked going around and sniffing things…

...a bit like Jimmy's dog...

…but only if it smells good!

When Dani has picked some flowers for her
teacher she walks back with the dog.

Jimmy thanks her and asks if she'd like to sit
down and chat, but Dani is in a bit of a hurry.

Chapter 12

Dani has to finish the present for her teacher! She dashes inside with the flowers and hunts for the book in her bulging backpack.

She turns to the page where she'd finished writing in the classroom.

The last time I was happiest, it read.

That was it! That was where she had got up to.

If only she could think what to write next.

She starts thinking so hard her brain creaks again. Although you can't hear it.

The only sound is Grandma's voice in the living room. She's talking to someone on the phone.

Grandpa is there too, interrupting.

Dani doesn't listen. She takes one of the flowers she's picked and holds it thoughtfully under her nose...

Grandma calls her exactly at that moment.

"Dani!" she calls. "Listen to this! I've asked
Ella's mother if you can go with them to their
summer island!"

Dani stares at Grandma.

"Would you like to?" asks Grandma.

What a question!

Would Dani like to go with Ella?

Her best friend in the whole world!

To an island for the summer!

The island Ella always talks about.

Where you can build huts.

And swim!

And sit on the edge of the cliff and dry off in the sun while you're looking for swimming deer.

Dani has never visited the island, but she's been wanting to go there her whole life. Without even knowing.

You can also row around it in a boat, Ella has told her.

And fish from the fishing cliff! For all kinds of fish. Perch and sole. And herrings with one i.

Of course Dani wants to go. Suddenly she feels a rush of happiness inside!

But it stops just as quickly.

"What about Dad?" she asks.

But Grandma keeps talking. "They'll come and get you tomorrow evening."

"But what about DAD?" Dani repeats.

"We'll visit him on our way home from school," says Grandpa.

"So he can see how nice you look in your new dress," says Grandma. "He'll be so happy when he hears that you'll be with Ella for the summer."

"Do you think so?"

"I promise you! He'll get better much faster if he doesn't have to worry about whether you are having fun or not."

"But he'll miss me!" says Dani. "The whole time!"

"Yes, of course..."

"And I'll miss him!"

"There are telephones," says Grandma. "You can ring him every day and tell him all the fun things you're doing. That will make him feel better."

"That's right," says Grandpa. "It'll be like pure medicine for him."

Dani looks hesitantly from one to the other.

"But I need to talk to Dad first."

"Of course, we'll do that. Talk to Dad, then decide what you want to do," says Grandpa.

"Okay," says Dani. "I just need to write something first."

Because now she knows exactly how the book will end!

This is what she writes:

The last time I was happiest was when I heard that I might *be* going to stay with Ella on her island.

We have so much fun together, she and I.
I don't know why.
We are both quite alike.
We both have pierced ears!

We are both good at drawing.

We both have hamsters. But Ella only has one.
I hope she gets another one.

And we both think it is very difficult to imagine
the way space never ends. We get headaches
when we try...

Dani pauses and rests her hand. She doesn't usually write this much. Not all at once, anyway.

But now, that's enough.

Spit spot spun
Now my book is done
is how she finishes.

There. Now she can give it to her teacher.

She leaps up, runs to get the phone, and puts in the best phone number she knows: Ella's!

"There you are!" cries Ella, thousands of streets and roads away.

Dani laughs, even though her father has been run over and everything.

You wouldn't think you could tell just from a voice how happy someone is!

"My mother told me what happened," says Ella. "What horrible bad luck!"

Dani swallows and feels in her whole body how close she was to having horrible bad luck forever.

Then Ella tells her the good news that she has another hamster, called Roy.

"Is Roy as cute as Party Boy?" asks Dani.

"Cuter!"

When they've finished talking, it seems as if things are getting back to normal. At least a little bit.

Suddenly Dani remembers her father's voice.
   "Dani," he'd said to her. And then, *"Amore!"*
   Those words! You'd hardly believe that two words could mean so much!

"Now the summer can begin," she says to herself.
   "What did you say?" asks Grandma who has come in to get the phone.
   "I said: now summer can begin!"

This edition first published in 2015 by Gecko Press
PO Box 9335, Marion Square, Wellington 6141, New Zealand
info@geckopress.com

English language edition © Gecko Press Ltd 2015

First American edition published in 2015 by Gecko Press USA, an imprint of Gecko Press Ltd.
A catalog record for this book is available from the US Library of Congress.

Distributed in the United States and Canada by Lerner Publishing Group, www.lernerbooks.com

Distributed in the United Kingdom by Bounce Sales and Marketing, www.bouncemarketing.co.uk

Distributed in Australia by Scholastic Australia, www.scholastic.com.au

Distributed in New Zealand by Upstart Distribution, www.upstartpress.co.nz

A catalogue record for this book is available from the National Library of New Zealand.
First published by Bonnier Carlsen, Stockholm, Sweden
Published in the English language by arrangement with Bonnier Group Agency, Stockholm, Sweden

Original title: *Sist jag var som lyckligast*
Text © Rose Lagercrantz 2014
Illustrations © Eva Eriksson 2014

The cost of this translation was defrayed by a subsidy from the
Swedish Arts Council, gratefully acknowledged.

Translated by Julia Marshall
Edited by Penelope Todd
Typesetting by Vida & Luke Kelly, New Zealand
Printed in China by Everbest Printing Co Ltd, an accredited ISO 14001 & FSC certified printer

Hardback (USA) ISBN: 978-1-927271-90-2
Paperback ISBN: 978-1-927271-89-6
E-book available

For more curiously good books, visit www.geckopress.com